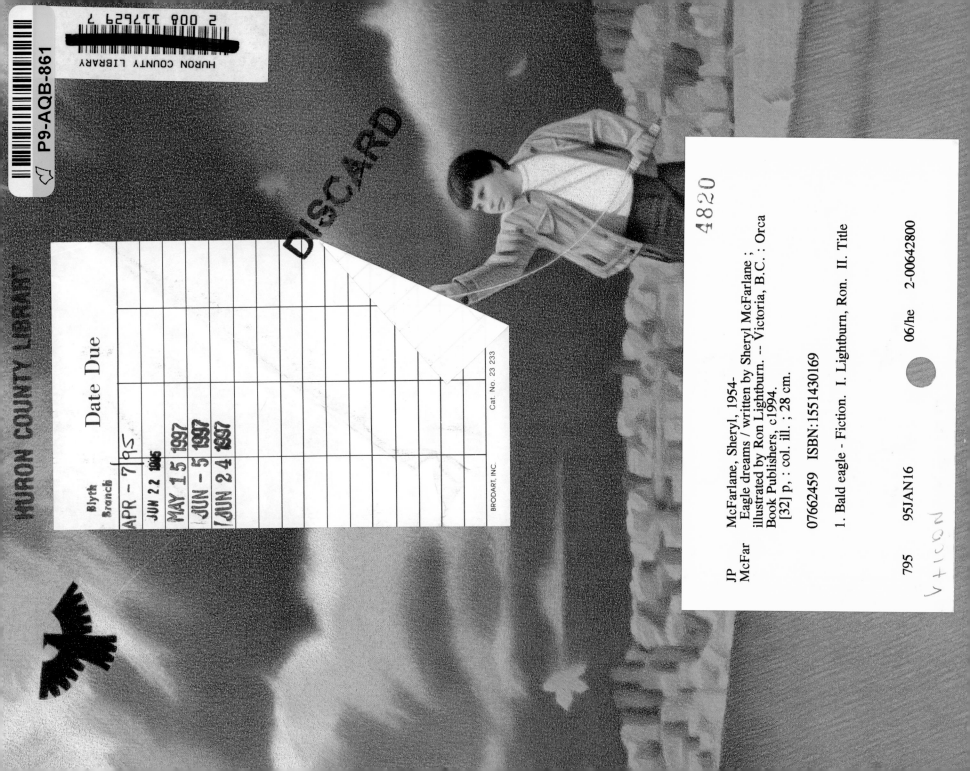

4820

JP
McFar

McFarlane, Sheryl, 1954-
Eagle dreams / written by Sheryl McFarlane ;
illustrated by Ron Lightburn. -- Victoria, B.C. : Orca
Book Publishers, c1994.
[32] p. ; col. ill. ; 28 cm.

07662459   ISBN:1551430169

1. Bald eagle - Fiction. I. Lightburn, Ron. II. Title

795   95JAN16   06/he   2-00642800

V + icon

EAGLE DREAMS

Written by
Sheryl McFarlane

Illustrated by
Ron Lightburn

ORCA BOOK PUBLISHERS

A damp chill lingered in the autumn air the day the veterinarian rattled up the driveway lined with leafless poplars. The farmer's son had found a bald eagle with a broken wing.

The farmer was waiting when the vet's truck pulled in. "Robin's got this foolish notion that we can keep the thing," the farmer muttered as he led the vet past fields that grew mud instead of winter rye. They climbed the hill where the forest met the farm. "The boy's a dreamer. Who has time for injured birds? This year I barely got my hay in."

That morning, before he'd found the eagle, Robin had leapt and twirled beneath the shadow of the fir so tall its bleached crown glinted silver in the sun. He'd spread his arms like the wings of eagles soaring overhead. And if someone had asked, he would have told them that he flew, at least inside his head.

Now as Robin waited, he shivered despite the warmth of the afternoon sun. "You'll fly again. I promise," he whispered to the injured bird.

"I kept the crows away," Robin proudly told the vet, when she reached the fir.

The eagle's wing was torn, a bone had snapped and its breathing came in ragged gasps. "It may not survive the shock," the vet explained.

The farmer shook his head. "Best to end its suffering." But Robin answered with a look as wild as the injured eagle's.

The weakened bird barely struggled when they wrapped it in a blanket. The vet reached into her bag. "Right now I'd say don't get your hopes too high."

The vet showed Robin how to splint the wing, explaining that its bones were far too fragile for plaster casts. As she worked, she talked about how eagles sometimes hit power lines when hunting for their prey.

"It's like tripping when you run to catch a ball. You're too busy looking up to check your feet." The vet glanced from the farmer to his son. "The wing is set, but the job is far from done. Now it will need constant care and feeding until its wing heals and those damaged feathers are replaced."

Robin's eyes glowed with willingness, but his father's eyes said no.

"I'll do my chores. I promise," Robin pleaded.

But the farmer remembered too many times when he had seen his son in the forest beyond the biggest barn, slipping on the mossy logs and rocks, while the garden went unweeded. Or running through the fields of golden corn and hay, while other boys his age helped with the threshing. Or swinging from a rope high above the ground, while the chickens went unfed.

T hen a shudder shook the giant bird to life and Robin cast a hopeful glance toward his mother.

"All right," the farmer sighed. "But you heard the vet, Son. Don't get your hopes too high."

Robin whooped and danced a rubber-booted jig before calming down to listen to the vet go through a list of things to do each day.

"One last thing," the vet warned. "That eagle's wild. It'll never make a pet."

A few days later, Robin and his mother drove out to see the ranger in the park. Eagles, gulls and crows lined the trees, waiting for a chance to pluck a tasty treat from the shallow waters of the spawning creek. Mother and son filled the truck with enough salmon to feed the injured bird all winter.

The eagle's home became a weathered cedar shed that kept out winter storms. The vet came by often to check up on the bird and on the boy.

By the end of winter holidays, the eagle's wing had healed enough to take the bandages off. The vet helped Robin move the bird to an unused bullpen shaded by the barn. Now there would be room to exercise its weakened wing.

At first his father grumbled about neglected chores, but Robin kept his promise. Sometimes he longed to climb to the swallows' nest above the hayloft or stalk the barnyard cat dozing in the sun. But when the cows stamped and swished their tails and mooed impatiently, Robin hurried over. And like his mother working down the line of cows, he'd soothe them with a gentle word or pat before milking. But his thoughts hovered over the eagle in his care.

There were no complaints about the eagle now, except from the barnyard geese who kept their distance from the bullpen.

Robin hauled a massive tree stump into the bullpen with the tractor. When the eagle's wing grew stronger, he watched the daily progress of its glide. Each day it gobbled up the fish and looked for more. It was hard work to satisfy an eagle's endless appetite.

One crisp morning when the smell of apple blossoms filled the air, Robin heard the bird's high-pitched squeal. An eagle circling overhead returned the call. It swooped down suddenly and Robin reached the pen in time to see a fish fall from the eagle's talons.

"Its mate," Robin's mother smiled. "It will stay nearby."

The eagle perched atop the stump like royalty.

Spreading massive wings, it glided to the ground. It would soon need a larger pen to build strength for the long flights essential for survival in the wild.

When the farmer volunteered the empty barn, Robin stared at his father in surprise. The farmer flashed a sheepish grin and mumbled something about a tractor that needed fixing.

T he next time the vet drove the driveway lined with leafy green, her truck kicked up a cloud of summer dust.

Robin led the way in silence, knowing that the eagle's time had come. But a smile touched the corners of his mouth when he peeked into the barn through a crack in the door. The eagle's crown of white shone majestic in the dusty light. And with its wings poised for flight, the eagle called out its anger at the constraints the barn imposed, not caring why but only when it was that it could go.

Robin swung the doors wide open and all of them — the vet, the boy, his father and his mother — watched the eagle swoop through the doors with a scream so full of wildness they could only stand in silence.

L ater in the day, Robin and his father climbed the hill that overlooked their farm. They sat beneath the shadow of the fir so tall its bleached crown glinted silver in the sun. And watched the eagle soar above their heads so high, calling to its mate.

"Will it be all right?" Robin asked.

The farmer hesitated before he reached out to his son and drew him near. "I hope so, Son," he said.

Robin sits at his bedroom window when the summer sun has given way to twilight stars. He sees the giant fir atop the hill where bald eagles often perch. He watches for their silhouettes against the sky when he should be asleep.

And in his dreams Robin flies with them above his father's fields of golden corn and hay and over cool green forests to the shoreline with its misty fogs that taste of salt and fish and seaweed.

To a world where bald eagles flourish
along with the dreams they continue to inspire.
S.M.

In memory of my father.
Thanks to Janice, Steve, Kevin, Tracy
and the Royal British Columbia Museum.
R.L.

Text copyright © 1994 Sheryl McFarlane
Illustration copyright © 1994 Ron Lightburn

Canadian Cataloguing in Publication Data
McFarlane, Sheryl. 1954-
    Eagle dreams

ISBN 1-55143-016-9 (bound).

1. Bald eagle—Juvenile fiction. I. Lightburn, Ron. II. Title.
PS8575.F39E2 1994   jC813'.54   C94-910366-7   PZ10.3.M32Ea 1994

Publication assistance provided by The Canada Council.
Story conceived by Ron Lightburn.
    Design by Ron Lightburn.

Printed and bound in Hong Kong

Orca Book Publishers
PO 5626, Station B
Victoria, BC Canada
V8R 6S4

10 9 8 7 6 5 4 3 2 1